The
Three
Little
Pigs

Modern Curriculum Press
BEGINNING
TO
READ
Series

Margaret Hillert

The
Three
Little
Pigs

illustrated by Irma Wilde

MODERN CURRICULUM PRESS
Cleveland • Toronto

ISBN 0-8136-5535-8 (paperback)
ISBN 0-8136-5035-6 (hardbound)

1 2 3 4 5 6 7 8 9   96 95 94 93

Here is a pig.

Here is a pig.

And here is a pig.

One, two, three.

Three little pigs.

10

Three funny little pigs.

See my house.

It is a little house.

It is yellow.

Little pig, little pig.

I want to come in.

You can not.

You can not.

You can not come in.

I can puff the house down.

Puff, puff, puff.

Here is my house.

It is a funny little house.

Little pig, little pig.

I want to come in.

You can not.

You can not.

You can not come in.

See me puff, puff, puff.

I can puff the house down.

Look here, look here.

My house is a big one.

It is red.

Little pig, little pig.

I want to come in.

Go away.

Go away.

You can not come in.

See me puff.

I can puff.

I can puff the house down.

23

See here, see here.

My house is not down.

I can go up, up, up.

I can go in.

Oh my, oh my.

It is funny.

You can not go up.

You can not come down.

And you can not come in.

Modern Curriculum Press Beginning-To-Read Books

Margaret Hillert, author of several books in the MCP Beginning-To-Read Series, is a writer, poet, and teacher.

The Three Little Pigs

The classic nursery story told in just 34 preprimer words with charming illustrations that carry the action of the story.

Word List

7	here		house	**15**	puff
	is		it		the
	a		yellow		down
	pig				
9	and			**19**	me
		13	I	**20**	look
10	one		want		big
	two		to		red
	three		come		
	little		in	**22**	go
	funny				away
		14	you		
12	see		can	**25**	up
	my		not	**26**	oh